Quentin Blake

MISTER MAGNOLIA

RED FOX

Some other books by Quentin Blake

All Join In
Angel Pavement
Angelica Sprocket's Pockets
Clown
Cockatoos
Fantastic Daisy Artichoke
The Green Ship
Loveykins
Mrs Armitage and the Big Wave
Mrs Armitage on Wheels
Mrs Armitage Queen of the Road
Quentin Blake's ABC
A Sailing Boat in the Sky
Simpkin
Zagazoo

MISTER MAGNOLIA
A RED FOX BOOK 978 1 849 41669 6

First published in Great Britain by Jonathan Cape,
an imprint of Random House Children's Books
A Random House Group Company

Jonathan Cape edition published 1980
Red Fox edition published 1999
This edition published 2010

3 5 7 9 10 8 6 4

Red Fox Books are published by Random House Children's Books,
61–63 Uxbridge Road, London W5 5SA

www.kidsatrandomhouse.co.uk

Addresses for companies within The Random House Group Limited can be found at:
www.randomhouse.co.uk/offices.htm

THE RANDOM HOUSE GROUP Limited Reg. No. 954009

A CIP catalogue record for this book is available from the British Library.

Printed in China

Mr Magnolia has only one boot.

He has an old trumpet

that goes rooty-toot —

And two lovely sisters
who play on the flute —

But Mr Magnolia has only one boot.

In his pond live a frog

and a toad and a newt —

He has green parakeets

who pick holes in his suit —

And some very fat owls
who are learning to hoot –
But Mr Magnolia
has only one boot.

He gives rides to his friends
when he goes for a scoot —

And the splash is immense
when he comes down
the chute —

But Mr Magnolia
has only one boot.

Just look at the way that
he juggles with fruit!

The mice all march past
as he takes the salute!

And his dinosaur!

What a MAGNIFICENT
brute!

But Mr Magnolia —
poor Mr Magnolia!
— Mr Magnolia
has
only one boot . . .

Hey —

Wait a minute . . .

Now then . . .

Keep going . . .

What's this?

Look!

It's a boot!

It's a boot!

Whoopee
for Mr Magnolia's
new boot!

Good night.